I WOULD LIKE TO DEDICATE THIS BOOK TO NICOLE GEIGER

AND TO THANK TAMARA RETTENMUND FOR HER HELP AND SUPPORT (R.C.)

FOR MY DAUGHTER, ADELAINE LOUISE VIRGINIA MUTH (J.J.M.)

BOOK DESIGN BY REMY CHARLIP • TYPOGRAPHY DESIGN BY TASHA HALL • HAND-LETTERING BY ERIC DEKKER

LIBRARY OF CONGRESS CATALOGING-IN-PUBLICATION DATA:
CHARLIP, REMY. WHY I WILL NEVER EVER EVER EVER HAVE ENOUGH TIME TO READ THIS BOOK / REMY CHARLIP ; PICTURES BY JON J MUTH.
P. CM. SUMMARY: A BUSY GIRL RECOUNTS ALL OF THE THINGS SHE HAS TO DO IN A DAY AS SHE TRIES TO FIND TIME TO READ.
ISBN 1-58246-018-3 [1. TIME—FICTION. 2. BOOKS AND READING—FICTION. 3. DAY—FICTION.] I. MUTH, JON J, ILL. II. TITLE.
PZ7.C3812 WH2000 [E]—DC21 • 99-052825 • FIRST PRINTING, 2000. PRINTED IN SINGAPORE • 1 2 3 4 5 6 7 — 04 03 02 01 00
TRICYCLE PRESS • P.O. BOX 7123 • BERKELEY, CALIFORNIA 94707 • WWW.TENSPEED.COM

WHY I WILL NEVER ever ever ever have enough time to READ THIS BOOK

Remy Charlip

PICTURES BY JON J MUTH

TRICYCLE PRESS • BERKELEY • CALIFORNIA

WHY I

I dreamed I had time
to read this book.
(But... if tomorrow goes
like it did today,
I will never...
ever ever ever...
have enough time...
to read this book.)

Then I awoke and yawned and stretched...
turned over... then fell asleep again.
Woke up (uh oh... I'm late...
what an amazing dream I had).

THINK SHE FINISHED THE BOOK?

I got out of bed, put on my bathrobe,
put on my slippers, went to the bathroom,
let the shower run ('til the water got hot),
got out of my bathrobe,
got out of my slippers,
got out of my pajamas.
CAREFUL! DON'T GET THE BOOK WET!

CAREFUL! DON'T GET THE BOOK WET!

DID YOU WASH BEHIND YOUR EARS?

Then I shook a tower...
(oops, sorry... still sleepy)
took a shower.
Washed my hair,
got out of the shower,
dried off my body with a towel.
Dried off my hair.
Hung the towel up to dry.
Brushed my teeth,
brushed my hair,
put on my slippers again.
Put my bathrobe on again.
Took my pajamas
back to my bedroom.

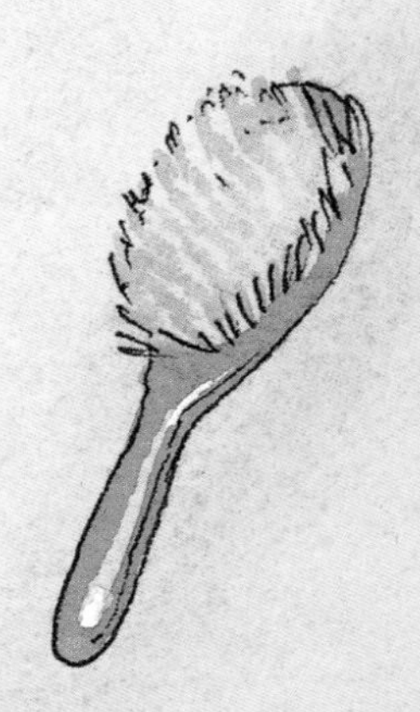

Hung up my *bathrobe*. Took off my slippers.
Put on some underwear. Put on some socks.
Put on a shirt. Put on my overalls.
Fluffed up my *pillow*.
Stuffed my pajamas under my pillow.
Made my *bed*.
Then I went to the kitchen
to make my breakfast.

Got out my bowl.
Put some cereal in it.
Cut up some banana over the top.
Put a few raisins all over that.
Poured some milk all over it *all*.
Took a big spoon
and ate it all up.

WHY I WILL NEVER
READ THIS BOOK
WHO LEFT THIS BOOK
IN THE FRIDGE?

Put back the milk, the cereal and the raisins, threw out the peel,

washed off my bowl, the knife and the spoon, cleaned off the table,

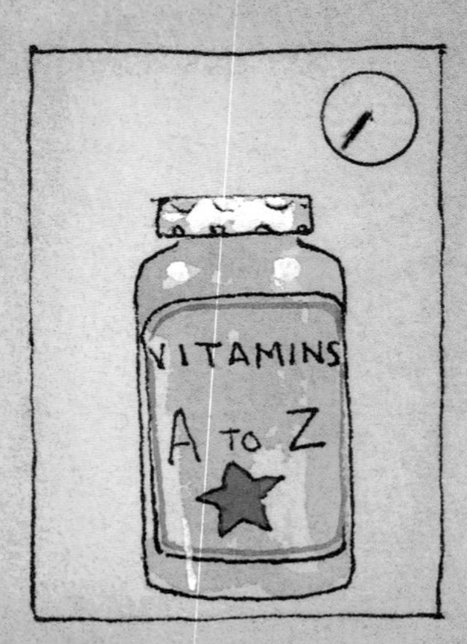

took my vitamins with a glass of water, put some tuna in a bowl,

mashed mayonnaise in, spread it on bread, packed it into a bag,

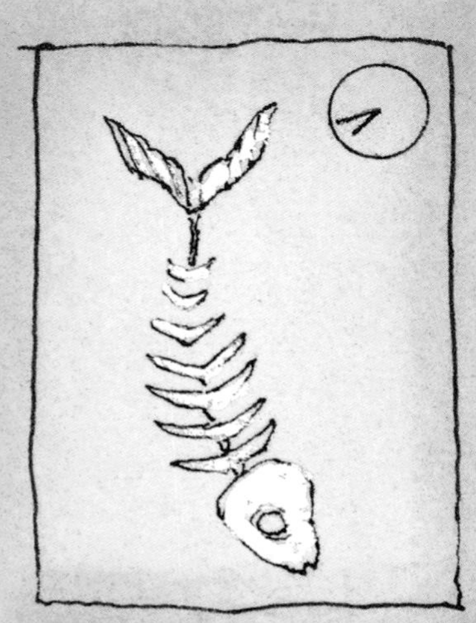

with a can of juice, fed my cat with some left over fish,

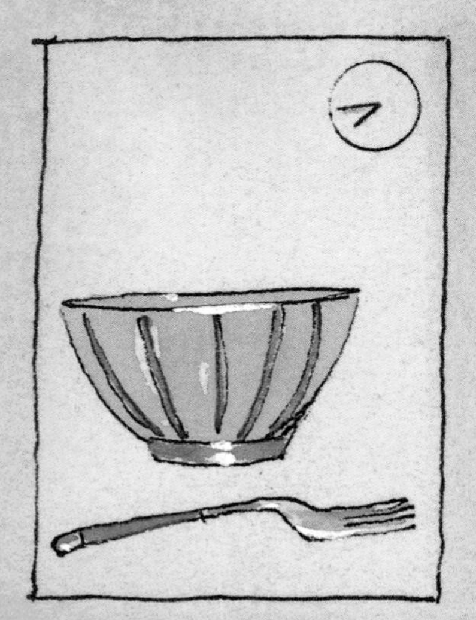

dumped the garbage, washed my hands, and the bowl and the fork.

Put on my boots.

Put on my sweater.

Put on my hat.

Put on my scarf.

Put on my coat.

Put on my mittens.

Put on my backpack.

Went to look for my book.

WHERE IS IT?
IT WAS RIGHT HERE!
IT'S GONE!
WHO TOOK IT?

HURRY UP!
WE'LL BOTH BE LATE!

Went to school. Did all kinds of things.

HOW DO YOU DIVIDE 7 APPLES AMONG 6 PEOPLE?
BUY A PEAR
I GIVE UP
MAKE APPLESAUCE

Then I came home, took off my coat,
my scarf and my hat,
wrote down what I did,
and still needed to do...
like patch a hole in my pants.
(They got caught on a nail.)

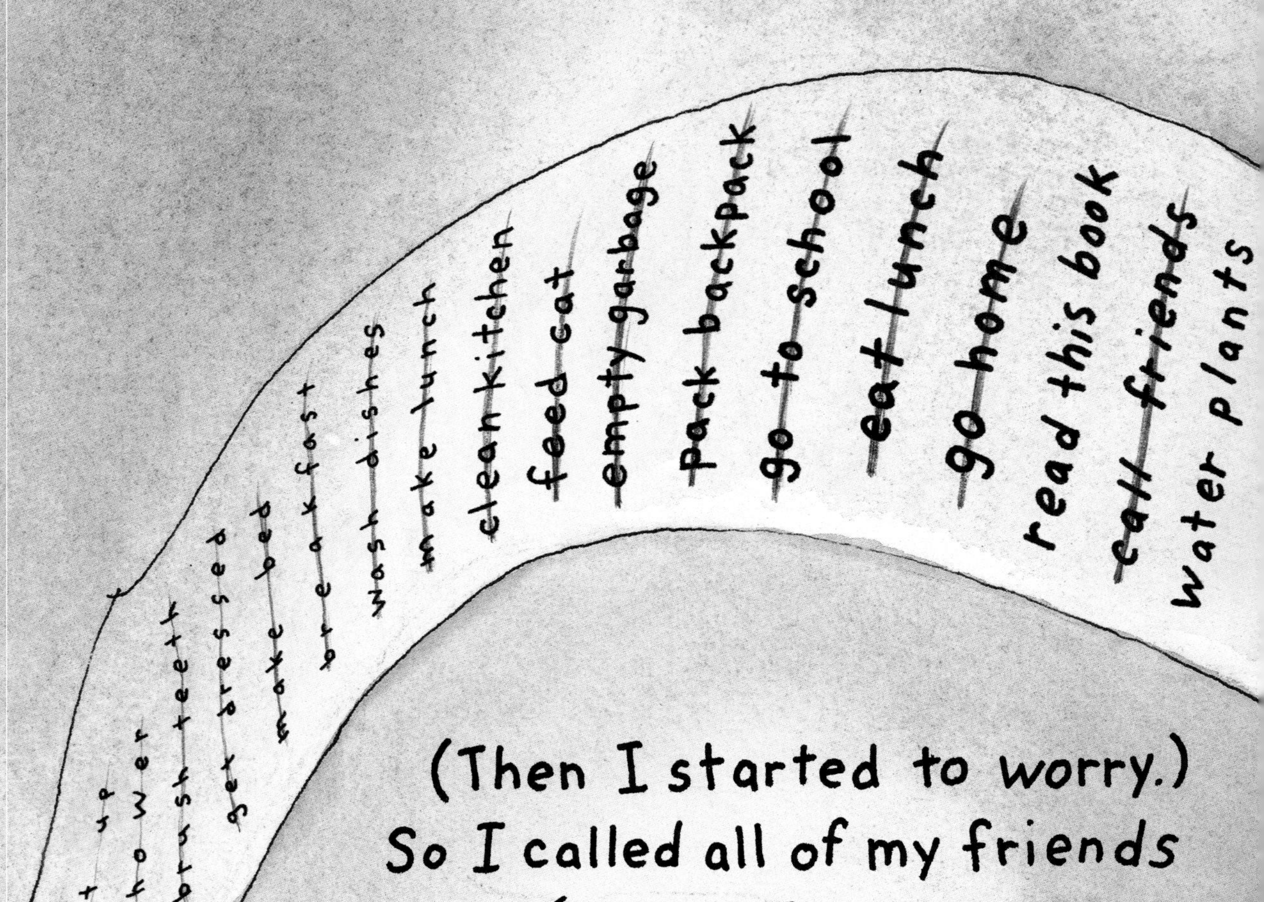

(Then I started to worry.)
So I called all of my friends
(to say I was worried,
that I would never... ever ever ever...
have enough time... to read this book).

CAN I USE THE PHONE NOW?
patch hole
baby sit
do homework
do exercise
wash bunny
set the table
eat dinner
read this book
go to bed

While father was cooking,
it was my turn
to watch the *baby*.

Then father said
come set the *table*.

CHIEF
COOK
AND
BOTTLE
WASHER

COOK
AND
BOTTLE
WASHE

When we sat down to eat,
I thought I could take
a quick look at my book.

MIGHT IT BE BETTER
TO READ YOUR BOOK LATER?
WHY I WILL NEVER
READ THIS BOOK

Then I really felt tired,
so I went back to my room,
took off my shoes and socks,
overalls and my shirt.
Put on my pajamas,
and opened the window.
Stuck my head out
(to smell the night air).

YOU LEFT YOUR BOOK ON THE TABLE

Then I turned down the covers
and crawled into bed.
I tried to read,
but was so tired,
I was falling asleep.

So you see... with all the things
I have to do every single day,
why I will never... ever ever ever...
have enough time... to read this book.

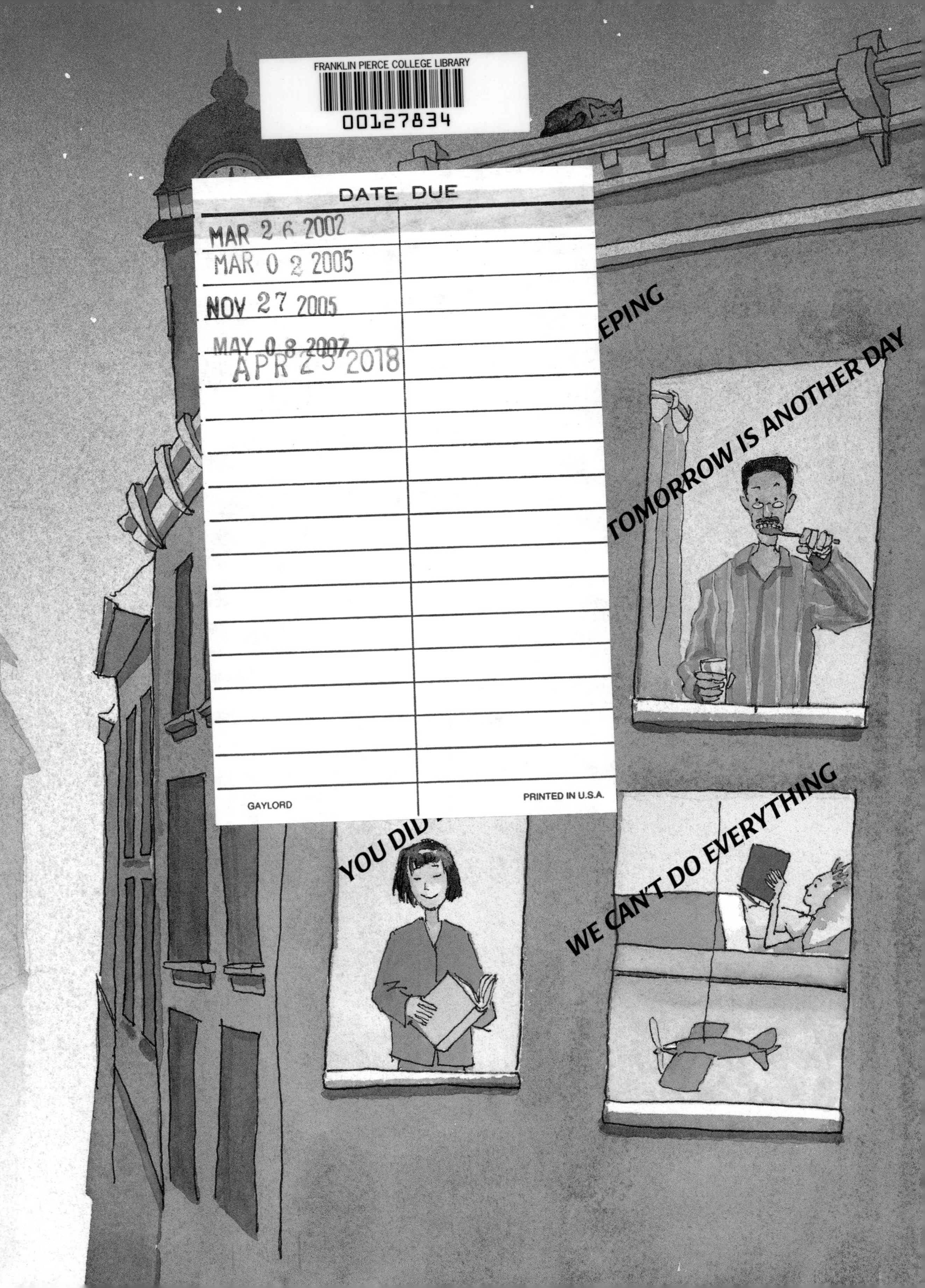
EPING
TOMORROW IS ANOTHER DAY
YOU DID
WE CAN'T DO EVERYTHING